HOPSCOTCH
TWISTY TALES

Little Bad Riding Hood

by Julia Jarman and Jane Cope

This story is based on the traditional fairy tale,
Little Red Riding Hood but with a new twist.
You can read the original story in Hopscotch Fairy Tales.
Can you make up a new twist of your own?

First published in 2010 by
Franklin Watts
338 Euston Road
London
NW1 3BH

Franklin Watts Australia
Level 17/207 Kent Street
Sydney
NSW 2000

Text © Julia Jarman 2010
Illustrations © Jane Cope 2010

The rights of Julia Jarman to be identified as the author
and Jane Cope as the illustrator of this Work have been asserted
in accordance with the Copyright, Designs and Patents Act, 1988.

A CIP catalogue record for this book is available
from the British Library.

ISBN 978 1 4451 0179 8 (hbk)
ISBN 978 1 4451 0185 9 (pbk)

Series Editor: Melanie Palmer
Series Advisor: Catherine Glavina
Series Designer: Peter Scoulding

Printed in China

Franklin Watts is a division of
Hachette Children's Books,
an Hachette UK company
www.hachette.co.uk

Once upon a time there
was a naughty girl called
Little Bad Riding Hood.

One day, her mother said,
"Take these cakes to your granny,
dear, and try to be good.

Go straight there and don't
speak to any strangers."

Little Bad Riding Hood set off,
but soon wandered off the path
and met a tall, grey stranger.
"Mmm … cakes," said the wolf.
"They look delicious."

GRANNY'S

"Hands off – they're for my granny!" said Little Bad Riding Hood, trying to be good.

"But she won't miss one, will she?"
said the wolf. Suddenly he heard
a noise and ran off.

9

Little Bad Riding Hood walked on,
but thought about the wolf's words.

She ate one
little cake ...

then another ...

and another!

"Crumbs!" cried Little Bad Riding
Hood when all the cakes had gone.
"What can I give Granny?"

She looked around and put
stones in her basket instead.
"Perhaps Granny won't notice,"
she thought and hurried on.

Meanwhile, at Granny's cottage, the wolf was busy. He tied Granny up and hid her.

He put on her nightcap.

He jumped into her bed.

He made up a tasty menu.

At last there was a knock at the door. "Granny, may I come in?" called Little Bad Riding Hood.

"Yes, my dear," the wolf replied,
pretending to be Granny.

"Oh, Granny!" said Little Bad Riding Hood, "you look very ill. What big eyes you've got!"

18

"All the better to see you with,"
said the wolf. "Now give me
the cakes!"

"But Granny," said Little Bad Riding Hood, "you look terrible. What a big nose you've got!"

"All the better to smell you with," said the wolf.

Now give me the cakes.

"But Granny," said Little Bad Riding Hood, "what a big mouth you've got."
"All the better to eat you with," said the wolf.

23

"Take them," said Little
Bad Riding Hood,
"but you won't like them."
Wolf grabbed the basket
and started to eat.

25

CRACK went his teeth as they crunched on the stones!

crunch!

crack!

"OUCH!" cried the wolf as his teeth fell out.

He ran away, toothless!

"Well done, Little Bad Riding Hood!" said Granny. "The wolf won't be eating anyone for a while. But why were you bringing me a basket of stones?"

As Granny looked round, Little Bad Riding Hood was already running out of the door!

Puzzle 1

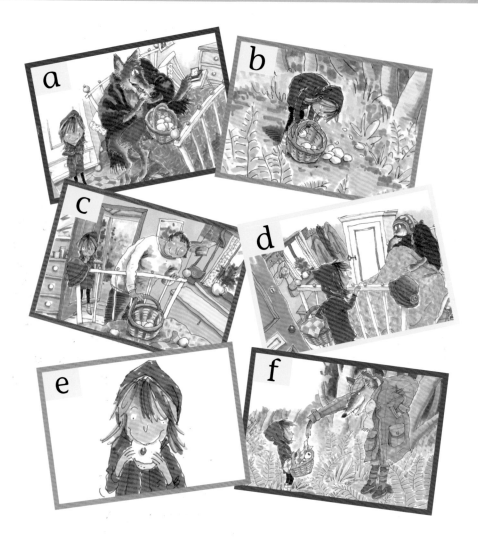

Put these pictures in the correct order.
Which event do you think is most important?
Now try writing the story in your own words!

Puzzle 2

Choose the correct speech bubbles for each character. Can you think of any others? Turn over to find the answers.

Answers

Puzzle 1

The correct order is: 1f, 2e, 3b, 4d, 5a, 6c

Puzzle 2

Little Bad Riding Hood: 3, 6

The wolf: 2, 5

Granny: 1, 4